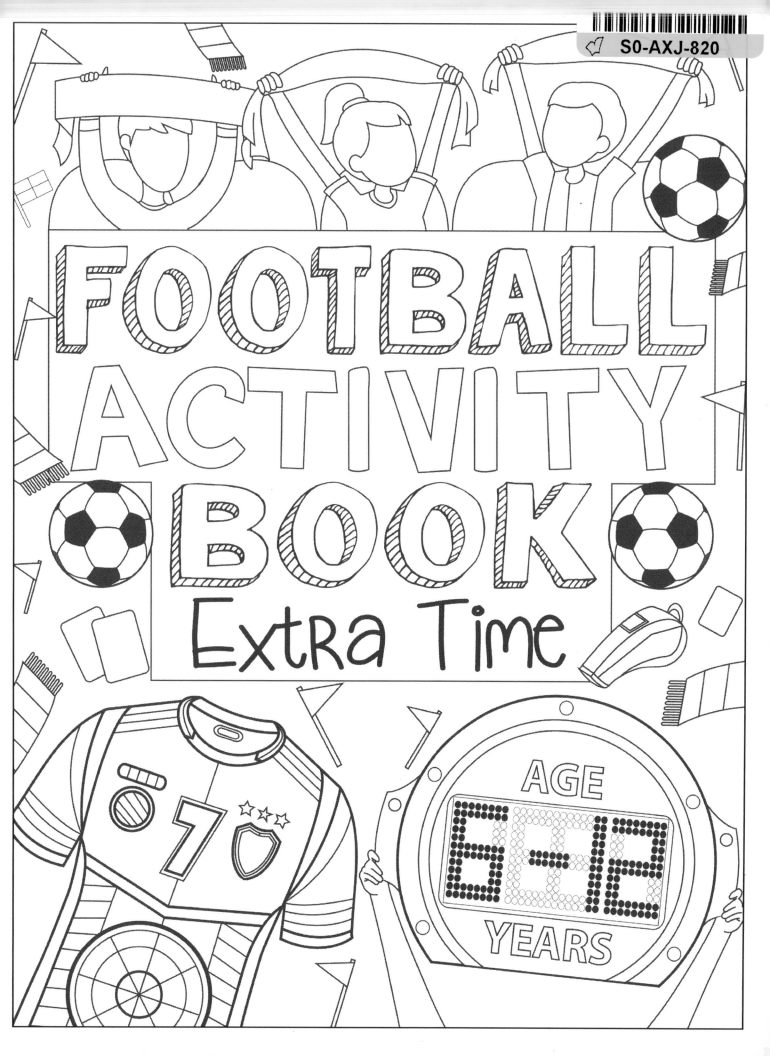

FOOTBALL ACTIVITY BOOK

Extra Time

AGE ☐☐ YEARS

Published in 2019 by The Future Teacher Foundation

© The Future Teacher Foundation

www.thefutureteacherfoundation.com

ISBN-13: 9781796420944

For printing and manufacturing information please see the last page.

If you choose to remove pages for framing, ask an adult to carefully extract with a scalpel and ruler.

Warning: This book is not suitable for children under 36 months of age due to potential small parts - choking hazard.

This book belongs to...

_____

Add words, patterns and colour to this picture...

Don't worry if you think you aren't a good artist, just do your best and have fun!

MAKE SURE YOU DRAW ON THE FANS' FACES AND ON THE ADVERTISING BOARDS TOO.

Colour this cool football shirt!

Spot the 11 differences between these two pictures.
Colour the picture when you have found them all!

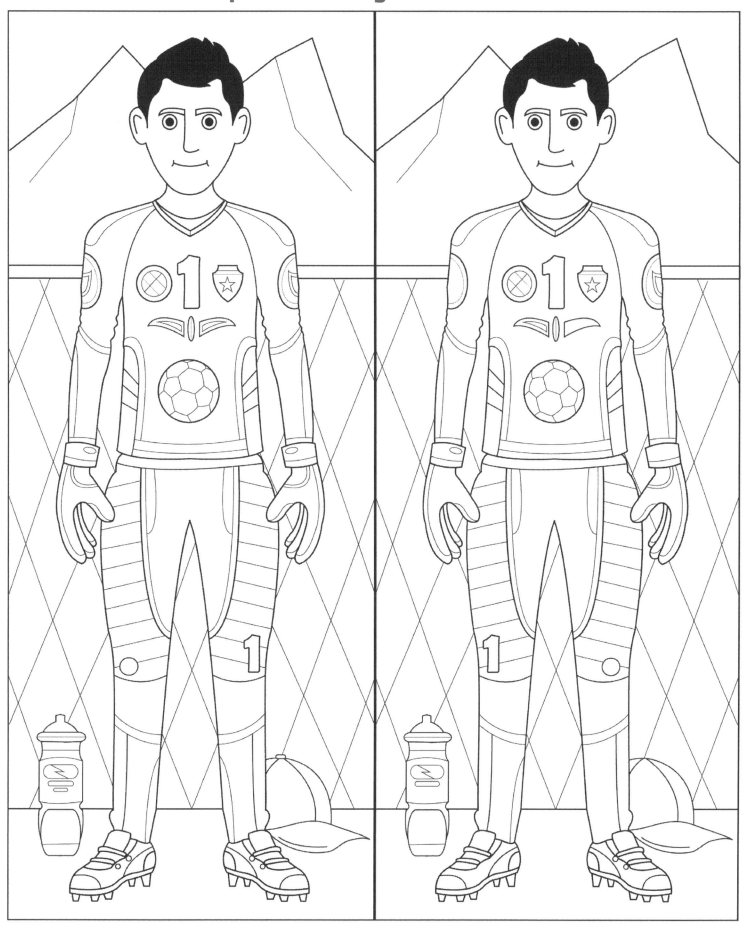

Design football cards for you and your friends!

Don't worry if you think you aren't a good artist, just do your best and have fun...

Maya Mate

Star Player

My School F.C

£50m

Midfield. Left footed. Scores goals.
Good tackler. Great passer.

These kids have lost their ball!

Help them get their ball back by finding a way through this maze...

NOW COLOUR THE KIDS AND THE BALL IF YOU WANT TO.

Fill in this A-Z of football words.

You can pick any word you like that has anything to do with football!

1 POINT FOR EACH WORD YOU CAN LIST.

A. _____

B. _____

C. _____

D. _____

E. _____

F. _____

G. _____

H. _____

I. _____

J. _____

K. _____

L. _____

M. _____

N. _____

O. _____

P. _____

Q. _____

R. _____

S. _____

T. _____

U. _____

V. _____

W. _____

X. _____

Y. _____

Z. _____

World cup winners word search!

V	B	S	P	A	I	T	I	T	I	B	V	S
S	G	R	U	R	U	G	T	T	R	U	R	P
R	O	N	A	S	D	B	A	A	A	R	A
G	E	R	F	Z	I	D	I	X	U	I
E	N	N	R	E	I	T	G	I	G	T
R	G	I	A	W	F	L	A	P	U	A
M	V	A	M	C	R	E	H	L	A	L
A	R	P	C	P	A	D	S	C	Y	R
N	K	S	E	E	N	G	L	A	N	D
Y	E	N	G	U	C	D	T	S	N	J
D	W	A	R	G	E	N	T	I	N	A

URUGUAY   GERMANY   ENGLAND   ARGENTINA

FRANCE   ITALY   BRAZIL   SPAIN

What are these commentators saying to each other?

Write what they are saying in the speech bubbles and then colour the picture when you are done!

Draw the other half of this football shirt!

Don't worry if you think you aren't a good artist, just do your best and have fun...

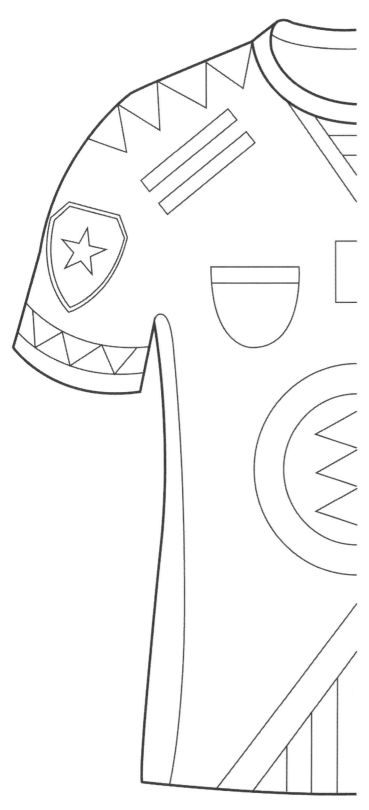

Now add some colour to the shirt.

Colour these cool boots any way you like!

Are they muddy or clean?

Draw and colour a football daydream!

Oh no! This boy is having a football day dream when he should be listening to his teacher. Draw and colour what you think he is dreaming about...

Design a new kit with your name on the back!

First, decide if this is for your school team, your local club side or a team you support that you dream of playing for. Next, add your name and squad number to the back of the shirt and then lastly, design the cool new kit...

Front

Back

Play the penalty shoot-out dice game!

You will need: a pen or pencil, dice (or an online dice) and ideally, someone to play against, but you can play this by yourself...

How to play...

Just like a real penalty shoot-out, take it in turns to try and score a penalty. You must decide who is going in goal first and who is taking the penalty first. Penalty taker rolls first. Goalie then rolls the dice. If the goalie rolls a higher number, then the penalty is saved! If the goalie rolls a lower or equal number, then a goal is scored. Draw a mini-football in the box if a goal is scored and draw a big X if the penalty was saved.

Normal penalty shoot-out rules apply – best of 5 and then sudden death!

PENALTY	1	2	3	4	5	6	7	8	9
Player 1									
Player 2									

USE THE BLANK PAGES IN THIS BOOK TO PLAY MORE PENALTY GAMES IF YOU WANT.

Colour these cool goalie gloves any way you like!

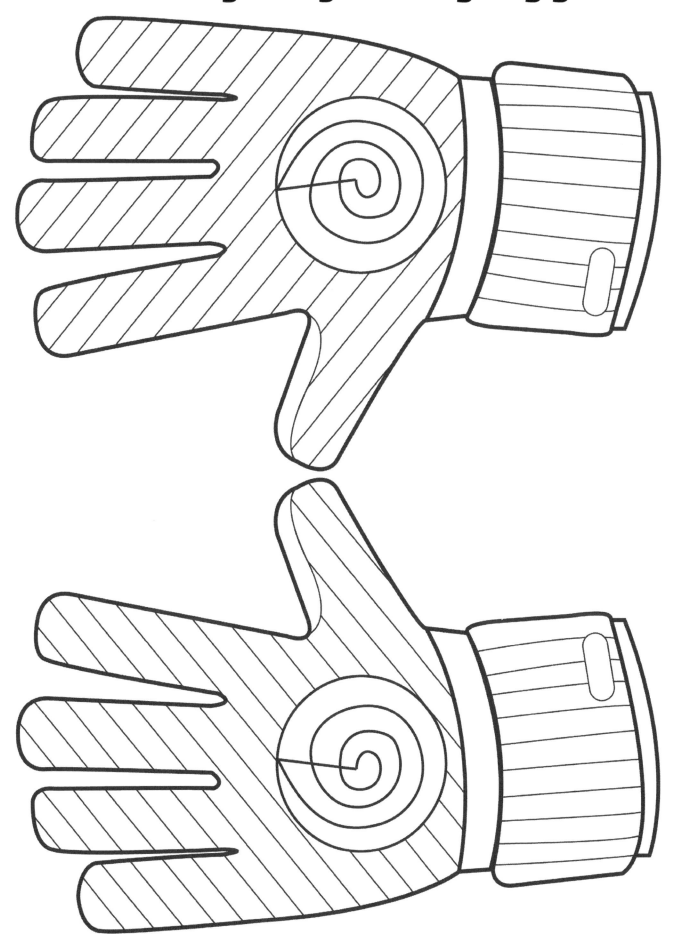

Predict the next football scores!

Choose your favourite professional league and then use the internet or a newspaper to find some of the next matches.

See if you can guess the correct scores of the matches before they happen, then check your guesses against the actual final scores, after the matches have finished...

_____ [ ] VS [ ] _____

ACTUAL SCORE ⟶ [ ] VS [ ]

_____ [ ] VS [ ] _____

ACTUAL SCORE ⟶ [ ] VS [ ]

_____ [ ] VS [ ] _____

ACTUAL SCORE ⟶ [ ] VS [ ]

_____ [ ] VS [ ] _____

ACTUAL SCORE ⟶ [ ] VS [ ]

_____ [ ] VS [ ] _____

ACTUAL SCORE ⟶ [ ] VS [ ]

_____ [ ] VS [ ] _____

ACTUAL SCORE ⟶ [ ] VS [ ]

Did you guess the correct score of any matches?_____

Did you predict any correct winning teams?_____

International football teams A-Z.

How many international football teams can you name?

Ask an adult or search the internet if you aren't sure...

1 POINT FOR EACH TEAM YOU CAN NAME!

A. _____

B. _____

C. _____

D. _____

E. _____

F. _____

G. _____

H. _____

I. _____

J. _____

K. _____

L. _____

M. _____

N. _____

O. _____

P. _____

Q. _____

R. _____

S. _____

T. _____

U. _____

V. _____

W. _____

X. _____

Y. _____

Z. _____

Find the pairs of trophies.

When you find a pair draw a circle around each one, and then a line that joins the pair.

What would you take to a football match?

Imagine you are going to play a football match and can take a bag
full of all the things you might need.

Draw pictures of all of the items that would be in your bag...

Add cool colours and designs to these shin pads!

Don't worry if you think you aren't a good artist, just do your best and have fun...

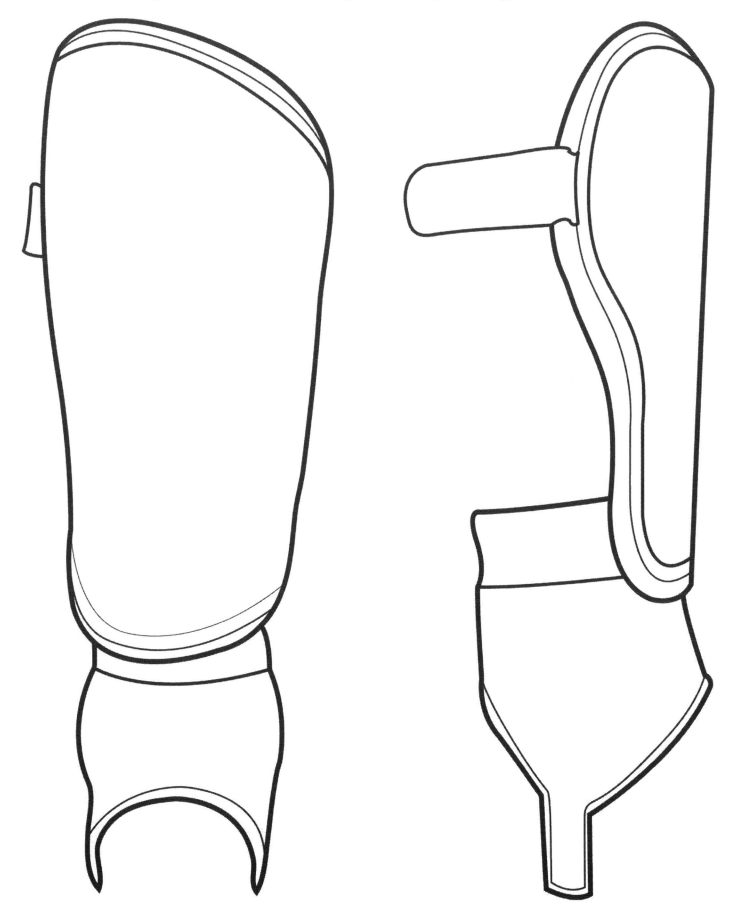

Use the grid to copy this picture...

Look closely and then copy the picture from the grid onto the other side.

Don't worry if it looks a bit tricky – just do your best and have fun!

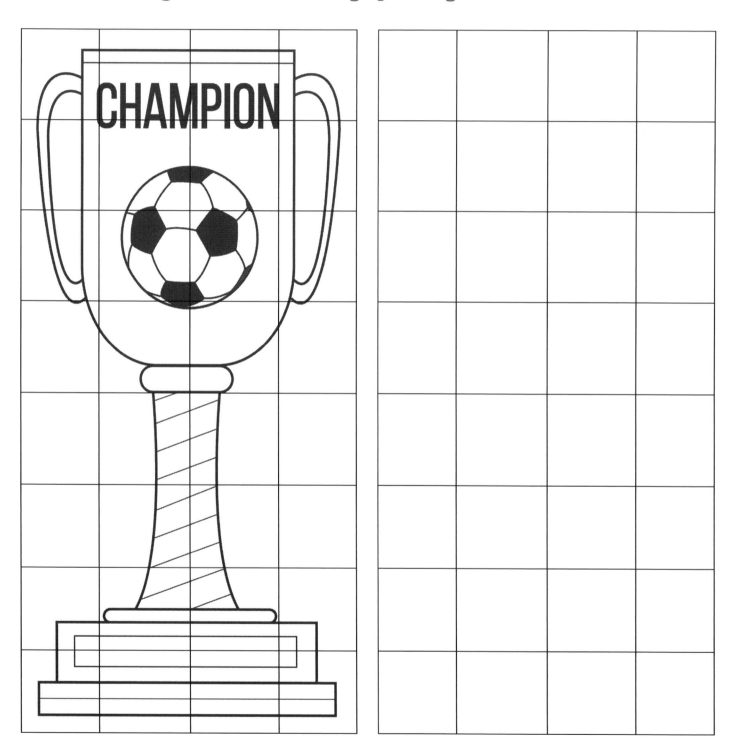

CHAMPION

NOW COLOUR THE PICTURES IF YOU WANT TO.

Design and colour a new training track suit for your favourite team!

Don't worry if you think you aren't a good artist, just do your best and have fun...

Can you solve these famous footballer anagrams?

You must try and work out who the professional footballer is.
For a bonus point can you write what teams they play for?

COLOUR THE SHIRTS WHEN YOU ARE DONE!

drazah
10

obgap
6

moars
4

_ _ _ _ _ _ _   _ _ _ _ _ _ _   _ _ _ _ _ _ _

alash
11

ruesaz
9

drocim
10

_ _ _ _ _ _ _   _ _ _ _ _ _ _   _ _ _ _ _ _ _

Can you find the football words in this word search?

A	W	P	A	T	T	A	C	K	S
L	I	D	S	U	D	F	O	U	M
E	N	E	E	B	E	N	A	H	I
F	G	F	T	F	Q	H	C	C	D
T	E	E	L	C	E	M	H	N	F
B	R	N	I	N	J	N	C	E	I
A	E	I	L	A	O	G	C	B	E
C	I	N	J	U	R	Y	S	E	L
K	S	W	E	E	P	E	R	U	D
S	U	F	O	R	W	A	R	D	B

FORWARD   **LEFT BACK**   **MIDFIELD**   **BENCH**

ATTACK   **COACH**   **DEFENCE**   **SUB**

WINGER   **SWEEPER**   **GOALIE**   **INJURY**

My premier league all-star dream team.

Pick your ultimate team from players currently in England's premier league.

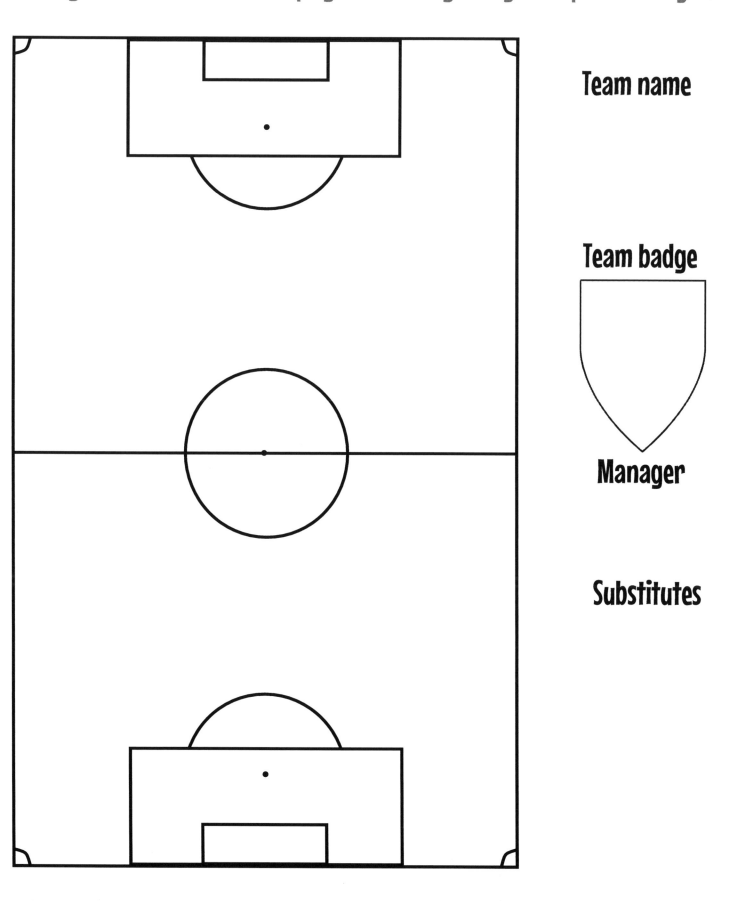

Team name

Team badge

Manager

Substitutes

Colour this mascot any way you like!

Create some new cards for a referee.

Referees use red and yellow cards. Your job is to create some new coloured cards to help a referee run a match.

Think about what colours to choose and what they might mean...

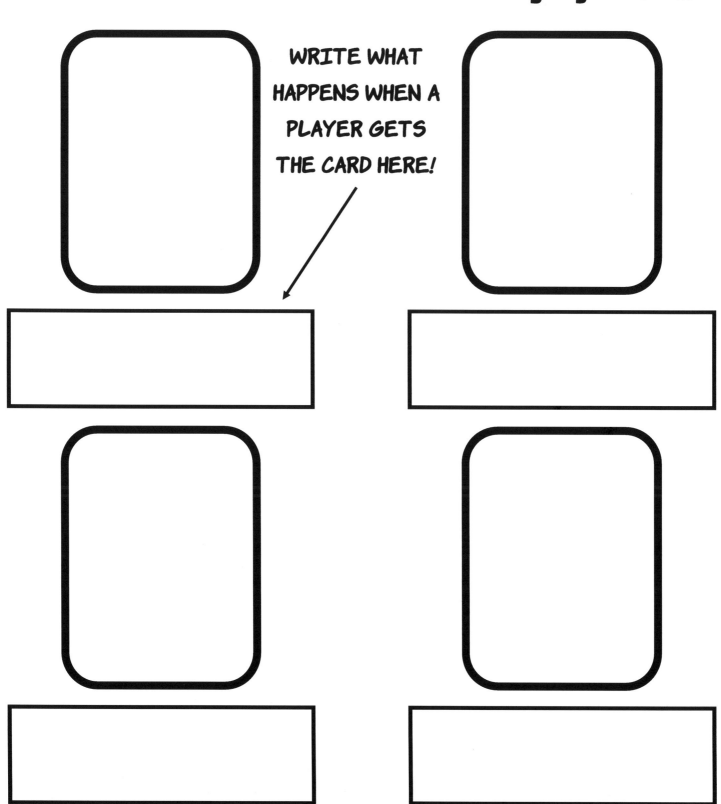

WRITE WHAT HAPPENS WHEN A PLAYER GETS THE CARD HERE!

Design a cool new away kit for your favourite team.

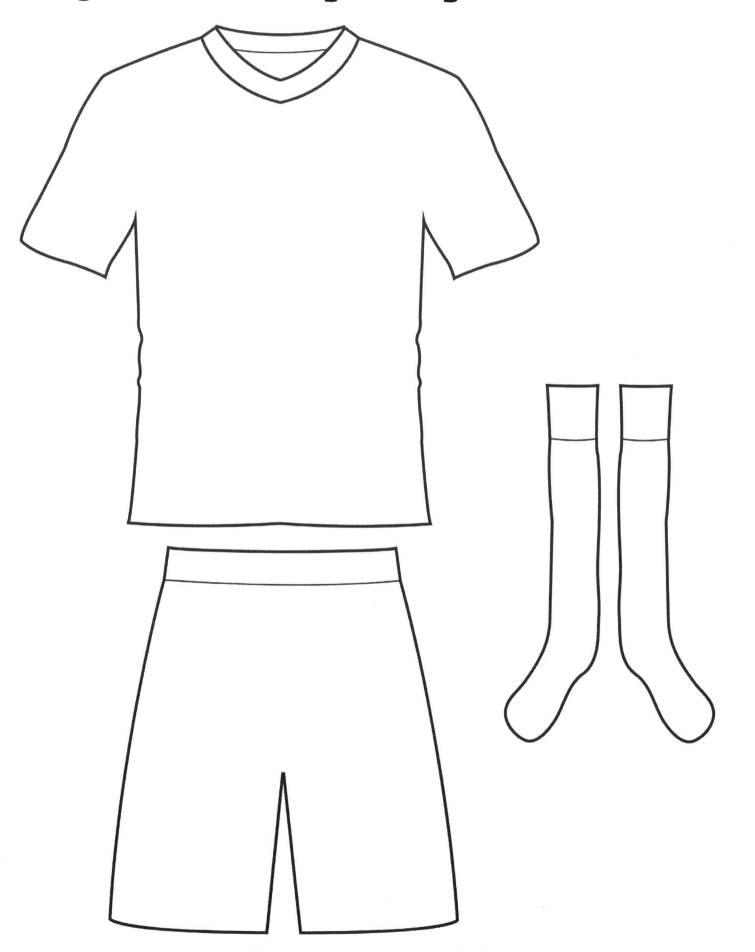

Imagine you've scored the winning goal in the world cup final.

Draw and colour a picture of you and your teammates celebrating your goal...

Don't worry if you think you aren't a good artist, just do your best and have fun!

Colour this referee page any way you like!

How many professional footballers can you name?

Use this page (and the blank pages afterwards if you need) to write the names of EVERY professional football player you can think of.

When you are finished, count them all up and write the total in the rosette below...

Made in the USA
San Bernardino, CA
15 December 2019